DIAL BOOKS FOR YOUNG READERS
Published by the Penguin Group
Penguin Group (USA) LLC
375 Hudson Street
New York, New York 10014

USA / Canada / UK / Ireland / Australia / New Zealand / India / South Africa / China
penguin.com
A Penguin Random House Company

Library of Congress Cataloging-in-Publication Data • Agee, Jon, author, illustrator. • It's only Stanley / Jon
Agee. • pages cm • Summary: Very strange noises that keep awakening the Wimbledon family one night
have an even stranger source. • ISBN 978-0-8037-3907-9 (hardcover) • [1. Stories in rhyme. 2. Dogs—Fiction.
3. Humorous stories.] I. Title. II. Title: It is only Stanley. • PZ8.3.A2594Its 2015 • [E]—dc23 • 2013042652

Manufactured in China on acid-free paper • 10 9 8 7 6 5 4 3 2 1
Designed by Lily Malcom • Text set in Neutraface Slab Text

Jon Agee

IT'S ONLY STANLEY

Dial Books for Young Readers

an imprint of Penguin Group (USA) LLC

The Wimbledons were sleeping.
It was very, very late,
When Wilma heard a spooky sound,
Which made her sit up straight.
"That's very odd," said Walter.
"I don't recognize the tune . . . "

"It's only Stanley," Walter said.
"He's howling at the moon."

The Wimbledons were sleeping.
It was later than before,
When Wendy heard a clanking sound
Below her bedroom floor.
"That's very odd," said Walter.
Then they heard another *clank!*

"It's only Stanley," Walter said.
"He fixed the oil tank."

The Wimbledons were sleeping.
It was even later still,
When Willie smelled a funky smell
That made him kind of ill.
"That's very odd," said Walter,
"When it's almost half past two!"

"It's only Stanley," Walter said.
"He's making catfish stew."

The Wimbledons were sleeping.
It was late as it can get,
When Wanda heard a buzzing noise
That made her all upset.
"That's very odd," said Walter,
"When it's almost half past three!"

Bzzz
Bzzz
Bzzz

Bzzz
Bzzz
Bzzz

"It's only Stanley," Walter said.
"He fixed our old TV!"

The Wimbledons were sleeping.
It was late beyond belief,
When Wylie heard a splashy sound
That made him say: "Good grief!"
"That's very odd," said Walter,
"When we've had so little rain!"

"It's only Stanley," Walter said.
"He cleared the bathtub drain."

Now Wilma wasn't happy.
And the children threw a fit.
"We'll never get to sleep tonight
If Stanley doesn't quit!"
"I understand," said Walter,
"And I'll talk to him right now."
But just as Walter turned to go,
There was a big—

The Wimbledons went flying,
Including Max, the cat.
Wendy looked around and said:
"Well, what on earth was that?!"
"I'll go and look," said Walter,
"And I'll be back very soon."

"It's only Stanley," Walter said.
"We're going to the—"